Too Many Babies

Mrs Tailless was a tenrec.*
She was worn out.
She was like the old woman
who lived in a shoe
(except *she* lived in a cave).
Mrs Tailless had so many children
she didn't know what to do.
Mrs Tailless had *thirty-one* babies!

Thirty-one mouths to feed.
Thirty-one faces to wash.

Thirty-one babies
to tuck in each night.
And Mrs Tailless had to do it
all on her own.

There was Mr Tailless, of course.
But Mr Tailless didn't know
about babies.
Mr Tailless was a teacher.
He knew all about children.
He had thirty-one
in his class at school.
But he didn't know
about babies.

Mr Tailless told his wife
she should teach the babies
to read,

to count to ten,

to tell the time,

to write their names.

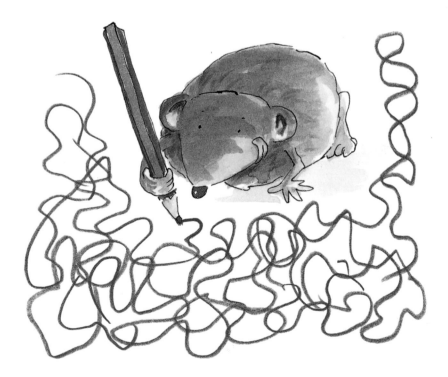

But poor Mrs Tailless
was too busy
to teach them anything.

One day she said to her husband,
"It is hard work, minding babies."
Mr Tailless said,
"Not as hard as teaching,
my dear."

"Perhaps we should
swop for a day," said Mrs Tailless.
"Then we would see which is harder."
"Very well," said her husband.
So that is what they did.

Next morning, very early,
Mrs Tailless went to work.
Mr Tailless stayed in bed.
He was looking forward
to a nice easy day.

Suddenly he heard a noise. Bump!
Then another. Bump!
And another.
Bump! Bump! Bump!

The babies were awake.
They were climbing out of bed
and falling down the stairs
like skittles.

Mr Tailless picked them up
and put them back in bed.
He ran up and downstairs
fifteen times.
He was puffed out.

"Now," said Mr Tailless, "no one must get out of bed until I say so."

But the babies kept on
climbing out of their beds
and falling downstairs.
In the end Mr Tailless gave up.

It was well past their
breakfast time.
The babies were hungry.
Mr Tailless put on
a big pan of porridge.

He put the babies in their chairs.
He gave each baby a spoon.
The babies banged their spoons.
The noise was terrible.
"Stop that noise, this minute,"
said Mr Tailless.

But the babies were
having a good time.
They went on banging.
Mr Tailless took the spoons away.
The babies began to cry.
The noise was terrible.

Mr Tailless noticed a smell.
The porridge was burning.
He stirred all the burnt bits in.
Mr Tailless thought the babies
wouldn't notice.
But they did.
The babies took one mouthful
and began to cry.

One or two began to throw
their porridge.
Then all the babies
threw their porridge.
Mr Tailless couldn't believe it.
He took the porridge away.
The babies began to cry *again.*

Now they were covered in porridge.
Mr Tailless had to bath them.
He filled the bath.
He lifted the babies
out of their chairs
and lined them up.
"Now stay there!" he said.

But the babies didn't know about
lining up.
Some of them climbed into the bath.
Some of them climbed
on the furniture.
Some of them rolled on the floor.
There was porridge everywhere.

Mr Tailless put each of the babies
back in its chair.
He was worn out
and it wasn't even break time.

He sat down for a rest.
"Peace at last," he thought.
But it didn't last.
The babies were bored.
They were crying again.

Mr Tailless thought he would
read them a story.
It was *The Tale of Peter Rabbit.*
He began to read to them.
But the babies didn't know
about rabbits.

They didn't know about beans
and radishes.
They didn't know about stories.
They couldn't even see the pictures.
The babies tried to climb out
of their chairs.
In the end Mr Tailless gave up.

Mr Tailless had been a teacher
for twenty years.
He had never had such
a difficult class.

Mr Tailless decided
to take the babies out.
He put the babies in their pram.
It was a special pram.
It held all thirty-one babies.

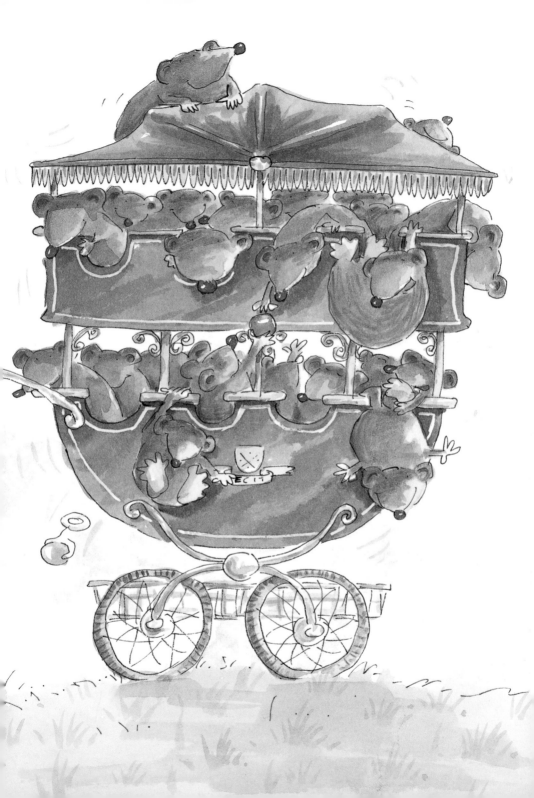

Now Mr Tailless felt happy.
"We will go to the park,"
he thought.

"The babies can have some exercise. It will wear them out. Perhaps they will sleep later."

Mr Tailless hoped he would be able to sleep too.

He pushed the babies in the pram. It was a long way, downhill.

In the middle of the park there
was plenty of space.
"The babies will be safe
here," he thought.
He lifted them out.
"Now, everyone must stay
where I can see them," he said.

But the babies disappeared
straight away.

They found trees to climb.

They found holes to fall down.

They found nasty things to eat.

They found good places to hide.
It took hours to find them all again.

The babies liked the park.
They didn't want to go home.
They began to cry.
The noise was terrible.

It was a long way back.
It was all uphill.
The babies didn't mind.
They slept the whole way.
But Mr Tailless was worn out.

When they got home
the babies woke up.
They had had a lovely sleep.
Now they were hungry.
But Mr Tailless hadn't made
any lunch.
The babies began to cry.
Mr Tailless felt like crying too.

"Babies are very hard work,"
he thought. "Harder than
children." Tomorrow he would be
glad to go back to school.

He put the babies in their chairs.
He gave each of them a biscuit.
He sat down in *his* chair
and fell asleep.

Soon Mrs Tailless came home.
She had had a lovely day.
The children were happy
to have a new teacher.
They liked to hear stories
about the thirty-one babies.
And all the tricks they got up to.

But Mrs Tailless had missed
her babies.
She wouldn't want
to leave them *every* day.

"No, one day a week
would be nice," she said.
"After all, a change
is as good as a rest."
But Mr Tailless was too busy resting
to say anything.

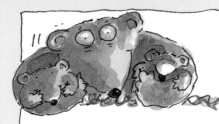

Crack-A-Joke

What do jelly babies wear
in the rain?
Gum boots!

Where do baby apes sleep?
In apricots!

What do you do
if a baby falls
down a well?
**Get a book about
bringing up babies!**

Little bundles of fun!

Doctor, Doctor,
my baby's swallowed
a bullet!
**Well, don't point
him at me!**

Who's that at the door?

A man pushing a pram.

Oh, tell him to push off!

ANIMAL
CRACKERS

COLLECT ALL THE
ANIMAL CRACKERS BOOKS!

A Birthday for Bluebell	978 1 40830 293 4	£4.99
Too Many Babies	978 1 40830 294 1	£4.99
Hot Dog Harris	978 1 40830 295 8	£4.99
Sleepy Sammy	978 1 40830 296 5	£4.99
Precious Potter	978 1 40830 297 2	£4.99
Phew Sidney	978 1 40830 298 9	£4.99
Open Wide Wilbur	978 1 40830 299 6	£4.99
We Want William	978 1 40830 300 9	£4.99

All priced at £4.99

Orchard Colour Crunchies are available from all good bookshops, or can be
ordered direct from the publisher:
Orchard Books, PO BOX 29, Douglas IM99 1BQ
Credit card orders please telephone 01624 836000
or fax 01624 837033 or visit our internet site: www.orchardbooks.co.uk
or e-mail: bookshop@enterprise.net for details.
To order please quote title, author and ISBN
and your full name and address.
Cheques and postal orders should be made payable to 'Bookpost plc.'
Postage and packing is FREE within the UK
(overseas customers should add £2.00 per book).
Prices and availability are subject to change.